Snake, Inky, and Bee jump.

Help!
Is it a monster?
Eek!

Can it be big monster footsteps?

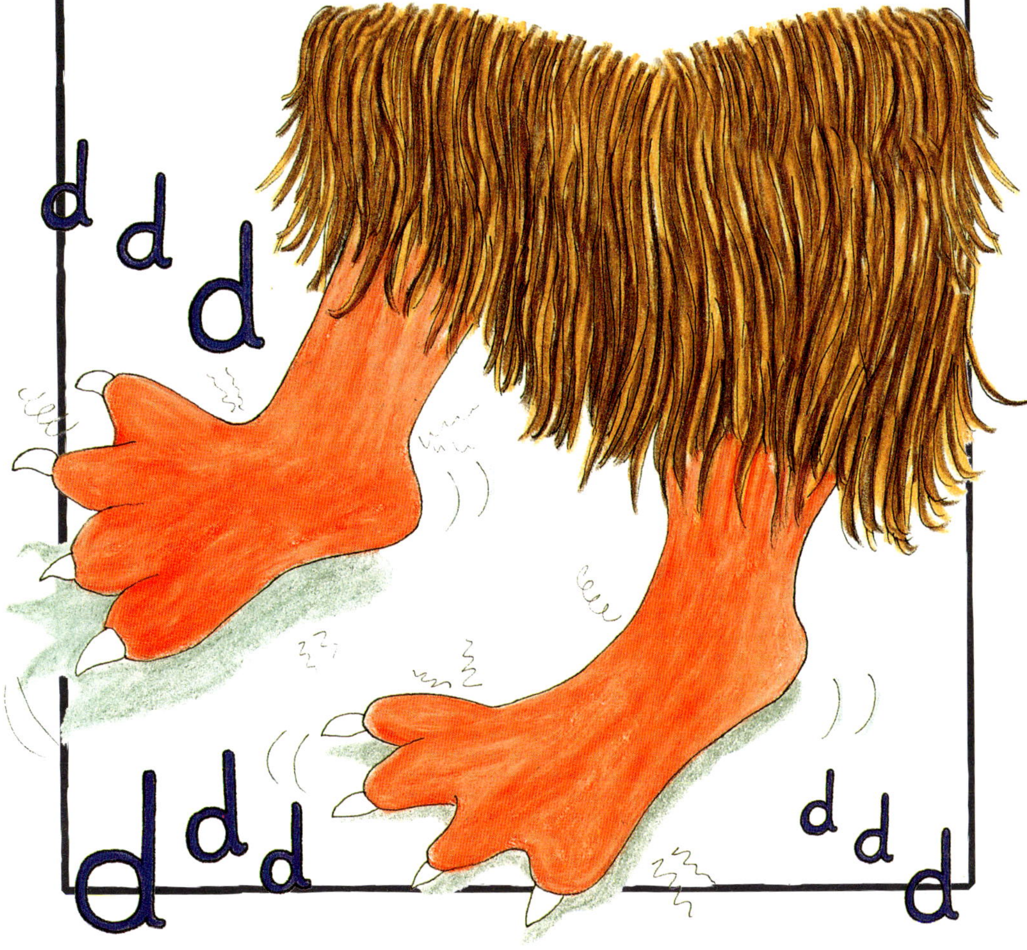

Inky, Snake, and Bee look around.

Under a tree
is a drum.

Bee, Snake, and Inky look up.

At the tree top
are three squirrels,
cracking nuts.

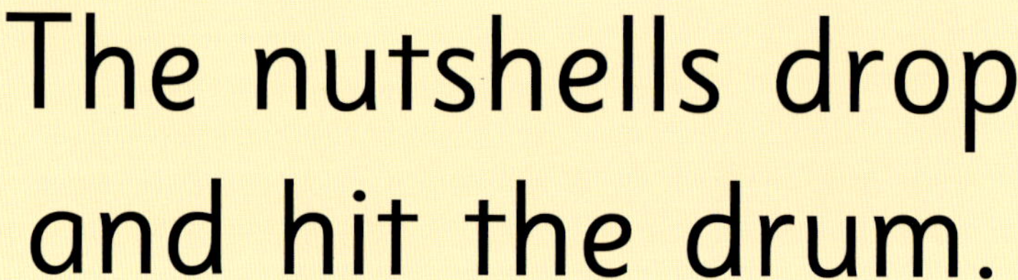

The nutshells drop and hit the drum.